THE STARS Will

# Still SHINE

By Cynthia Rylant

Illustrated by Tiphanie Beeke

HarperCollinsPublishers

this new year . . .

the sky will still be there

the stars will still shine

birds will fly over us

church bells will chime

cows will have calves

kittens will sleep

flowers will bloom

(a promise they keep)

we shall have peaches

we shall have pie

we shall have ice cream

three scoops high!

homes will be cozy

homes will be warm

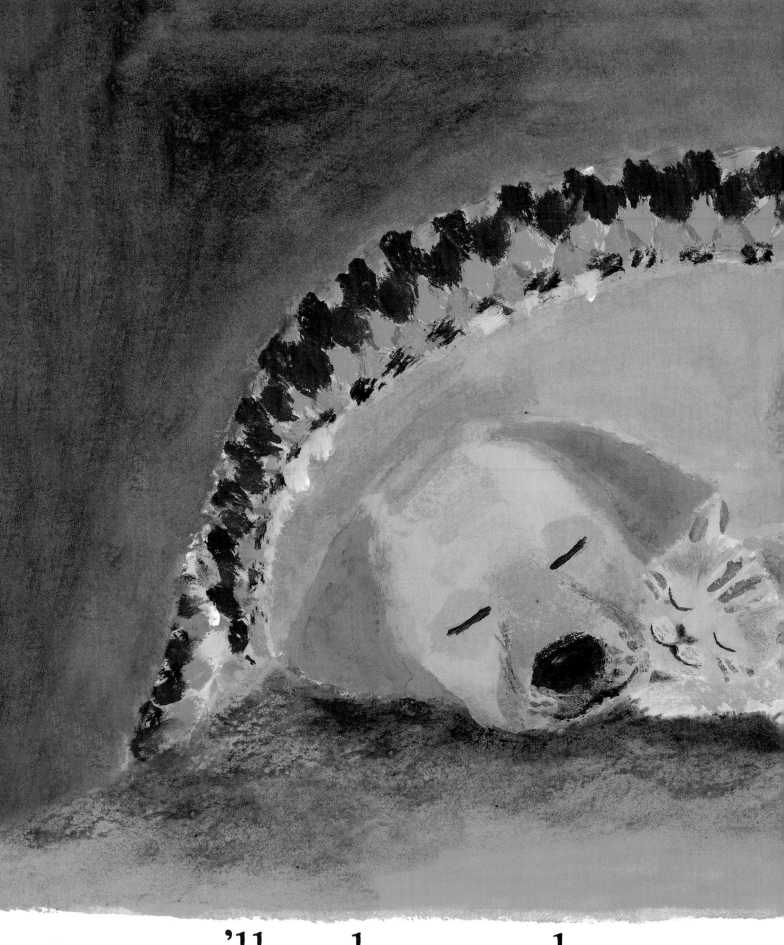

we'll curl up together

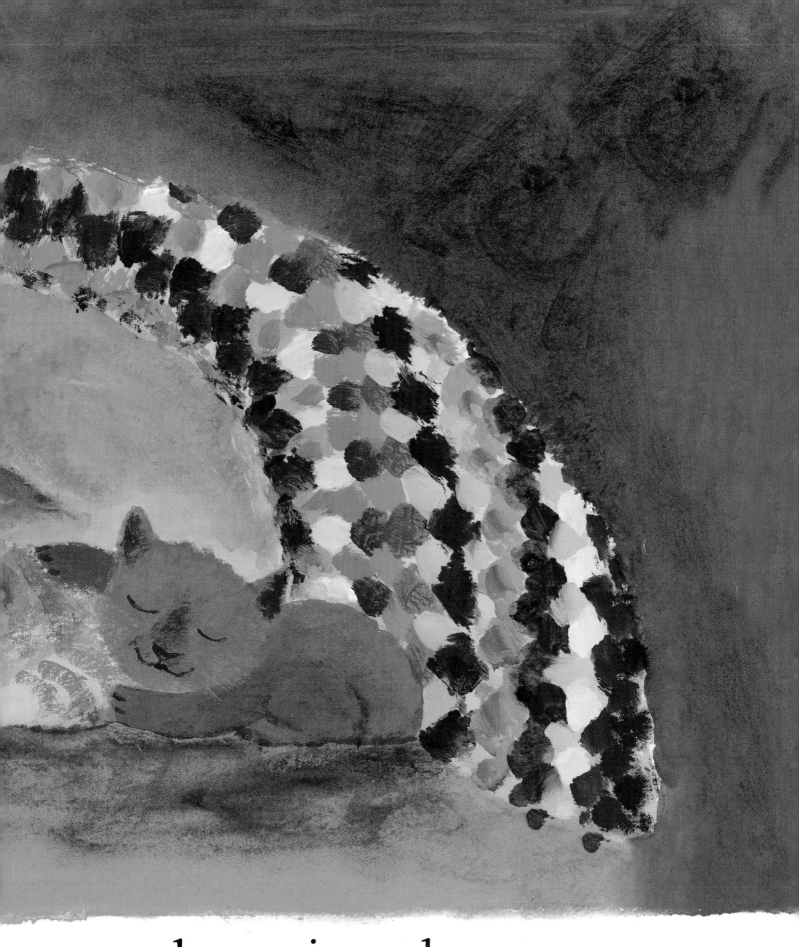

when rain makes a storm

and in this new year

love will be strong

growing and growing

all the days long

there will be goodness

there will be grace

there will be light

in every dark place

the sky will still be there

the stars will still shine

birds will fly over us . . .

church bells will chime.

The Stars Will Still Shine · Text copyright © 2005 by Cynthia Rylant · Illustrations copyright © 2005 by Tiphanie Beeke
Manufactured in China. All rights reserved. No part of this book may be used or reproduced in any manner whatsoever
without written permission except in the case of brief quotations embodied in critical articles and reviews. For information address
HarperCollins Children's Books, a division of HarperCollins Publishers, 1350 Avenue of the Americas, New York, NY 10019.
www.harperchildrens.com · Library of Congress Cataloging-in-Publication Data · Rylant, Cynthia. · The stars will still shine / by Cynthia
Rylant ; illustrated by Tiphanie Beeke.— 1st ed. · p. cm. · Summary: In pictures and rhyming text, this verse reassures the reader that life's
familiar things, such as stars that shine and sleeping kittens, will continue as they always have. · ISBN 0-06-054639-5 — ISBN
0-06-054640-9 (lib. bdg.) · [1. Security (Psychology)—Fiction. 2. Stories in rhyme.] I. Beeke, Tiphanie, ill. II. Title. · PZ8.3.R96St
2005 · 811'.54—dc22 · 2004014796 · Designed by Stephanie Bart-Horvath · 1 2 3 4 5 6 7 8 9 10 · ❖ · First Edition